BRICKS

The House a Greedy Pig Built

For my earliest reading partners, Harry and Freddy – K.C.

For Clementine Rose, with love – T.F.

American edition published in 2020 by Andersen Press USA,
an imprint of Andersen Press Ltd.
www.andersenpressusa.com

First published in Great Britain in 2020 by Andersen Press Ltd.,
20 Vauxhall Bridge Road, London SW1V 2SA.

Text copyright © Katie Cotton, 2020.
Illustration copyright © Tor Freeman, 2020.

Distributed in the United States and Canada by
Lerner Publishing Group, Inc.
241 First Avenue North
Minneapolis, MN 55401 USA

For reading levels and more information, look up this title at www.lernerbooks.com.

Library of Congress Cataloging-in-Publication Data Available
ISBN: 978-1-72841-578-9

Printed in China.
1–TOPPAN–7/1/2020

BRICKS

The House a Greedy Pig Built

Katie Cotton   Tor Freeman

Andersen Press USA

In a town, there was a pig
who'd come into some gold.
He had a truck and lots of clothes,
and owned some land (marked sold).

Pig thought the view was rather nice
and had a plan in mind.
So, one day, he drove to town,
to see who he could find.

He found a cat whose job was roofs.

For bricks he found a pup.

A hen said, "I can do the wood."

"Good," said Pig. "Now listen up!"

"I want a home that's very grand,
that's big and tall and fine.
I'll give you all four of these coins
to build this house of mine."

They each said yes and off they went
for bricks and planks and glass.
They slaved away, all night and day,
till it was built at last.

The house was painted white and blue
and was a sight to see!

It had four rooms
but Pig thought, "Hmmm.
That's not enough
for me."

"It isn't big," he told them all.
"Add stables and a shed.

And once that's done you'll have your coins.
Fair is fair," he said.

So off they went to get more bricks

and stone that weighed a ton.

They sawed and smashed and
banged and crashed

until Pig's home was done.

The house now had a shed and porch,
and a conservatory!
It had eight rooms but Pig thought, "Hmmm.
That's not enough for me."

"It isn't tall," he told them all.
"Build high above my head.
And when that's done, you'll have your coins.
Fair is fair," he said.

So off they went to get more bricks

and up and up it soared.

It had TWELVE rooms, a swimming pool,
and a golden door.

When it was done, the house stood tall
and big and fine and grand.
It was a splendid house, in fact,
the best house in the land!

And sure enough Pig's face lit up.
He clapped his hands with glee.
"Oh yes," he cried. "Yes, that's the one.
Yes, THAT'S the house for me."

"I thank you for your work," he said. "And here's your hard-earned pay. These four gold coins are yours to share. Now please be on your way."

Hen clucked. Cat hissed. Dog barked and said, "There's some mistake I feel. You said you'd give us all four coins, so twelve coins was the deal."

"No, 'all' means coins for you to share," said Pig. "That's what I said. As you've done well I'll give two more.

Fair is fair—"

...but off they sped.

The pig was pleased.

"Wow, what a house!

And built for half the price!

I'm such a clever pig," he thought,
"to get a house so nice."

Pig went inside and shut the door.
He soon turned off the light.
In bed asleep he dreamt of gold
and snored throughout the night.

When morning came the pig awoke
and stumbled for the stairs.

He stopped to scratch his bum and stretch,

then stepped into midair!

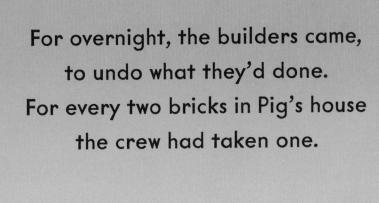

For overnight, the builders came,
to undo what they'd done.
For every two bricks in Pig's house
the crew had taken one.

"You said twelve coins would be the fee.
You gave us six instead.
And so we're taking half the house.
Fair is fair," they said.

The house swayed left.
The house swayed right.
The walls gave quite a creak.

"Help me," cried Pig,
"I'll give you more!"
as he began to shriek.

It might not have been fatal if
the house was not so big.
But seven thousand bricks came down...

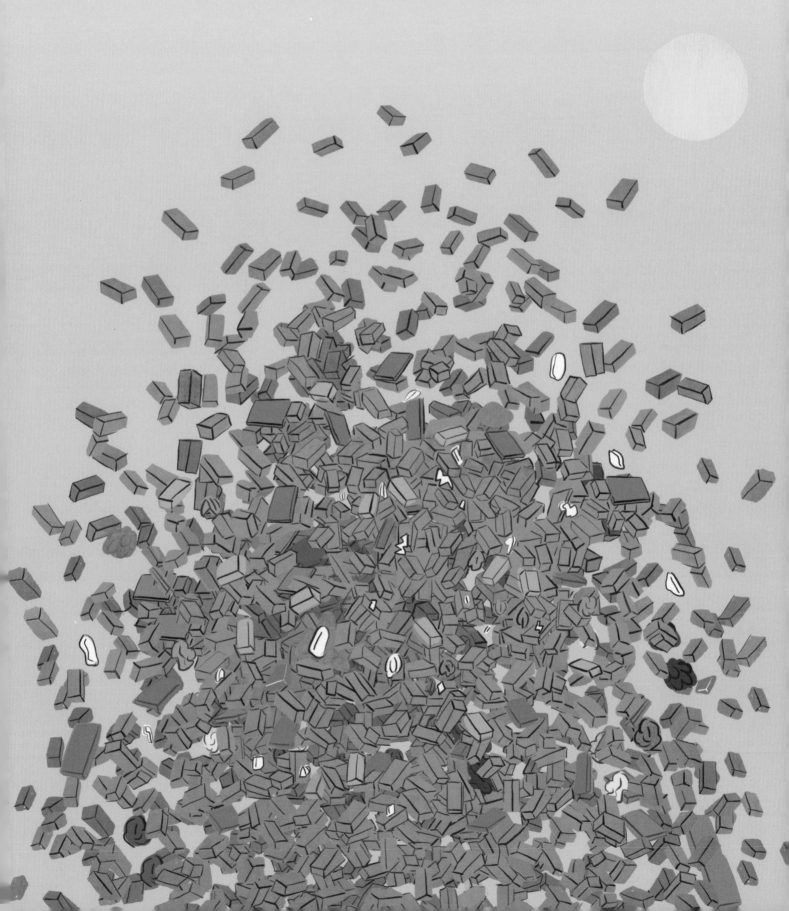

And that was that for Pig.